First published in 2008 by Simply Read Books
www.simplyreadbooks.com

Text © 2008 Elizabeth James Illustrations © 2008 Atanas Matsoureff

LIBRARY AND ARCHIVES CANADA CATALOGUING IN PUBLICATION

James, Elizabeth, 1958-
The woman who married a bear / Elizabeth James ; Atanas,
illustrator.

ISBN 978-1-894965-49-1

1. Indians of North America–British Columbia–Pacific
Coast–Folklore–Juvenile literature. 2. Folklore–British Columbia–
Pacific Coast–Juvenile literature. 3. Bears–Folklore–Juvenile
literature. I. Matsoureff, Atanas II. Title.

PS8569.A4335W64 2008   j398.209711'0452978   C2007-906743-3

We gratefully acknowledge the support of the Canada Council for the
Arts and the BC Arts Council for our publishing program.

Book design by Elisa Gutiérrez

10 9 8 7 6 5 4 3 2 1

Printed in Singapore

THE WOMAN WHO MARRIED A BEAR

retold by Elizabeth James

illustrated by Atanas

SIMPLY READ BOOKS

I T WAS THE END OF SUMMER. The blackberries were as black as night and as sweet as sunshine. "Another day of picking," grumbled a young, haughty girl as she and her friends left their village near the sea to journey up the mountain.

As she entered the alpine meadow—spluck—the girl stepped into a big pile of bear dung. "Yuck!" she cried. "Bears! Ugly, filthy bears!"

"Shh!" hushed one of her friends. "This is fresh. The bears are nearby. They might hear you."

"Don't be foolish," replied the girl. "Bears are just dumb animals."

When their baskets were full and the sun slipped behind the trees, the girl and her friends headed home.

SNAP! All of a sudden the red cedar strap of the girl's basket broke. Her berries spilled across the forest path.

"Leave them," said her friends. "It's getting dark."

"I'm not leaving these for the greedy bears to eat. I'll catch up to you. Go on."

Alone, the girl fixed her strap and picked up her berries. By the time she was done, the forest was silent and filled with shifting shadows. She shivered and hurried down the path.

SNAP! This time it wasn't her strap. It was the sound of a breaking branch. She spun around to face a man who was wearing a thick bear pelt.

"What are you doing out so late?" he asked.

"I was picking berries. I'm on my way home, to my village near the sea."

"It's too late to travel that far," he said. "My village is nearby. You must stay with us tonight."

She had no choice. She knew that she would get lost if she continued down the mountain in the dark.

The girl followed the man through the woods to a village she had never seen or heard of before. He led her towards curls of smoke and a warm orange-yellow glow. Many men and women dressed in bear pelts were gathered around a fire.

"Why are they wearing such heavy pelts in the summer?" she wondered.

They stopped in front of a very old man.

"So, nephew, you found the one who insults us," the Chief growled.

The young man whispered something in the Chief's ear.

The Chief looked at the girl and nodded. "She is beautiful. Although she deserves to be punished, you may take her for your wife."

Frightened, the girl fled from the fire. Just as she neared the edge of the village, a tiny woman jumped in front of her and squeaked, "Stop!"

It was Mouse Woman, the ever-watchful shape shifter who makes sure order is kept between humans and supernatural beings.

Mouse Woman seized the girl's cloak and pulled her into a longhouse. "Sit down!" she ordered in a shrill voice. "Your insults have angered the Bear People."

"They don't look like bears!" exclaimed the girl.

"Like me, the Bear People can transform back and forth from animal to human," replied Mouse Woman. "You are lucky the Chief's nephew wants to marry you. Now you must learn to respect your new family."

As suddenly as she had appeared, Mouse Woman vanished.

The girl buried her face in her hands. She could not imagine a worse punishment than marrying a bear.

To the girl's surprise, her bear husband was gentle and clean. He gave her many soft furs to sleep on and delicious foods to eat.

"He may seem kind, but truly he is selfish. He forced me to be his wife," she reminded herself.

Seasons came and went. In the summer the girl became pregnant. "My child will be an ugly bear. I will hate it," she thought.

Then, one day in late autumn, her husband took her aside. "Your brothers have been searching for you, and now they are close to our village. If they find us they will kill many bears. We must all leave right away."

"My brothers! If only I could see them," she thought. But she knew that her brothers weren't as powerful as the Bear People. If they found the bears, surely they would be the ones killed.

So she packed quickly and left Bear Village with her husband.

He led her high up into the mountains where nothing stirred. When she became too tired and cold to continue the journey, he carried her the rest of the way, to a cave on the side of a cliff.

In the cave, the girl gave birth to not one, but two tiny creatures. Neither bear nor human, they were a mixture of both, with human child faces and bear cub bodies. Despite their bizarre appearance, the girl fell in love with them at first sight. They snuggled next to her day and night, nursing with their eyes closed. She slept most of the time, too, and so did her husband. Many weeks passed. The babies grew bigger, their fur grew longer and softer, and soon they tumbled playfully around the cave. The girl forgot about her brothers.

Then, early one morning, she woke to faint shouts coming from the mountainside below. Leaving her husband and children asleep, she peered out of the cave's entrance and saw four specks: her three brothers and their hunting dog.

Now was her chance to escape. The girl waved her arms, but her brothers didn't see her. They were heading in the wrong direction. How could she get their attention? She grabbed a handful of snow, packed it into a tight ball, and threw the snowball at them with all her might.

The snowball rolled down the hill, coming to rest in front of her brothers' dog. As the dog sniffed it and began to bark, the girl's eagerness turned to hesitation at the thought of leaving her children.

"So they found you," came a voice from behind.

Filled with shame and dread, the girl turned to face her husband. Surely he would kill her brothers.

"Don't worry," her husband said, as if he could read her mind. "I saw in a dream that your brothers would find you. Because I love you, I will not harm them. If you love me, sing my death song and teach your people to respect the bears."

With those final words, her husband transformed into a bear and went down to face the men and their spears.

The brothers, amazed at how easily they had killed the giant bear, hurried up to their sister. "Don't cry now! We have saved you!"

But she didn't stop weeping. The brothers were bewildered until their sister's children emerged from the cave. They realized then just how closely she had been living with the bears. "Time to come home," they said gently.

"Only if you join me in singing my husband's death song," she replied.

When the song was done, they helped their sister down the mountain. Falling flakes melted and mixed with the tears on her cheeks. Her children followed far behind.

In the village near the sea everyone gathered in the
longhouse to welcome home the girl who was now a woman
and her strange children. Despite the celebrations and
the joy of being reunited with her friends and family, the
woman's heart ached. As she comforted her children, who
huddled by her side, she thought about how wrong she had
been to ever belittle the bears. They deserved great respect.

Over the years the woman taught the villagers to hunt the bears only when necessary and to do so with deep reverence.

She was happy to be sharing what she had learned, but she felt out of place, and so did her children. She often caught herself growling softly and craving raw salmon.

One day her brothers brought her three bear pelts to make into clothing for the coming winter. When they left, the woman stroked the fur, remembering her husband.

Impulsively, she placed one pelt on her back and the other two over her children. The woman's clothing melted away into the fur. She fell onto all fours, like her children. Hair sprouted over their faces. Within seconds, they had completely changed. The woman and her children were now three beautiful bears!

The bears gracefully ambled away into the mountains. They were never seen again.

THIS RETELLING OF THE TALE OF A GIRL who insulted and was taken by the bears is an ancient story of many First Nations cultures of the Yukon, Alaska, and British Columbia. The Haida, Tlingit, Tsimshian, Tagish, Tutchone, and Ahtna peoples each have different versions.

This particular retelling does not detail the relationship between the girl and Mouse Woman, which often includes an exchange of goods for advice. This retelling also ends with the girl returning to the bears, rather than staying in her village. The Haida people who live in Haida Gwaii off the West Coast of British Columbia tell a similar story sometimes titled *Bear Mother*. In *Bear Mother*, the young woman returns to her village and does not leave to go back and live with the bears, although her cub children do. She stays, marries, and gives birth to human children who establish the Haida Bear clan.

Tales of marriage between animals and humans are found in many different cultures and often include the transformation of an animal into a human. In *The Woman Who Married A Bear*, the human becomes an animal. This physical transformation, however, is secondary to the more important transformation, which takes place within the young woman's heart. Her beastly attitude towards the animal kingdom changes as she grows to respect and love her bear husband. The theme of respect and reverence for the animal kingdom is found in many First Nations tales.

This story celebrates the voices and the visions of all the great native storytellers of the past and present.